TOFFEE
and
Marmalade

TWO PET STORIES

Kes Gray
Linda Jennings

Illustrated by
Dee Shulman

OXFORD
UNIVERSITY PRESS

OXFORD
UNIVERSITY PRESS

Great Clarendon Street, Oxford OX2 6DP

Oxford University Press is a department of the University of Oxford.
It furthers the University's objective of excellence in research, scholarship,
and education by publishing worldwide in

Oxford   New York

Auckland   Cape Town   Dar es Salaam   Hong Kong   Karachi
Kuala Lumpur   Madrid   Melbourne   Mexico City   Nairobi
New Delhi   Shanghai   Taipei   Toronto

With offices in

Argentina   Austria   Brazil   Chile   Czech Republic   France   Greece
Guatemala   Hungary   Italy   Japan   Poland   Portugal   Singapore
South Korea   Switzerland   Thailand   Turkey   Ukraine   Vietnam

Oxford is a registered trade mark of Oxford University Press
in the UK and in certain other countries

British Library Cataloguing in Publication Data

Data available

ISBN 978-0-19-915204-9

1 3 5 7 9 10 8 6 4 2

Mixed Pack (1 of 6 different titles): ISBN 978-0-19-915200-1
Class Pack (6 copies of 6 titles): ISBN 978-0-19-915199-8

Printed in China by Imago

Contents

Crunch Time for Toffee

Kes Gray

Chapter 1

Toffee had been a bad dog.

She had eaten a whole bag of dog biscuits and it wasn't even her dinner time.

"Bad dog, Toffee!" said Dad.

"Bad, greedy dog, Toffee!" said Mum.

"Woof!" said Baby Andrew.

Mum, Dad and Toffee looked at Baby Andrew. He was sitting on the kitchen floor with a tennis ball in his mouth.

He dropped the ball on the floor and then barked again.

"Woof, Woof, Woof, Woof!" he yapped, as the ball rolled across the kitchen floor towards the empty bag of dog biscuits.

Mum looked at Dad. Dad looked at Toffee, and then everyone looked at Baby Andrew again.

Now he was lying on his back with his legs in the air, waiting for his tum to be tickled.

"Goodness gracious," said Mum. "It isn't Toffee that's eaten a whole bag of dog biscuits. It's Baby Andrew!"

Dad picked up the empty Doggybix bag.

"Read what it says on the packet," said Mum, in a bit of a tizz.

Dad put his reading glasses on and peered at the writing on the packet.

Baby Andrew's mum clasped her hand to her mouth.

Oh my word! They've brought out the dog in Baby Andrew!

"Woof, woof!"

Baby Andrew sprang on to all fours.

He scratched himself with his back leg and then scampered up the hallway.

"What else does it say on the packet?" said Mum.

Baby Andrew's dad lifted the small writing closer to his glasses.

"It says, '*For extra bounce and vitality*'," he said.

"Extra bounce and vitality? What does that mean?" said Baby Andrew's mum.

"I think *that's* what it means," said Dad, pointing down the hallway.

Baby Andrew was running round and round in circles, chasing his nappy.

He stopped for a moment and barked with excited eyes at Mum, Dad and Toffee.

Then he bounded up the stairs. Mum, Dad and Toffee bounded after him.

"What are we going to do?" said Mum, as Baby Andrew started scratching at the bedroom door.

"How are we going to stop him?" said Dad.

"There's no stopping him, now," thought Toffee.

Toffee was right. There was no stopping Baby Andrew.

All Mum, Dad and Toffee could do was watch, as Baby Andrew scampered from one room to another.

In the lounge, they found Baby Andrew chewing the sofa.

In the nursery, he gnawed the ears off his squeaky toys.

In the garden, he even chased the neighbour's cat up a tree.

"Sit!" said Baby Andrew's dad in desperation, as Baby Andrew started digging up the lawn.

"Heel!" said Baby Andrew's mum, as Baby Andrew ran into the house and did a puddle on the carpet.

"What are we going to do?" said Baby Andrew's mum. "He should be doing baby things, not doggy things."

Toffee wasn't so sure. She quite liked the idea of having another dog around the house.

"I know what we must do," said Baby Andrew's dad. "We must take him to the doctor."

"Yes, we must take him to the doctor," said Baby Andrew's mum.

And take him to the doctor they did.

The doctor looked long and hard at Baby Andrew's tongue.

"Does he always dangle it out of his mouth like that?"

"Only since he's been a dog," sighed Baby Andrew's mum.

The doctor continued his examination.

When he asked Baby Andrew to say, "Aah", Baby Andrew said, "Woof".

When he tried to look down Baby
Andrew's throat, Baby Andrew started
licking his face.

And when he tried to listen to his
chest, Baby Andrew rolled over on his
back and started panting, loudly.

"You need to take him to a vet," said
the doctor, folding up his stethoscope.

"Yes, we need to take him to a vet," said Baby Andrew's mum to Baby Andrew's dad.

So take him to the vet they did.

The vet lifted Baby Andrew up on to her table and gave him a careful examination.

"Is there a cure?" asked Baby Andrew's mum. "Can anything be done to make him better?"

The vet looked long and hard at
Baby Andrew.

"I'm afraid there is only one thing
I can suggest," said the vet.

Mum and Dad gasped. Toffee would have to go?

We can't get rid of Toffee. She's our dog. She's our little dog!! She's our lovely, good, Toffee dog!!!

But the vet was deadly serious.

"It's because Toffee is a dog that she will have to go. Baby Andrew is copying every doggy move she makes. As long as there is a dog in the house, Baby Andrew will never stop doing doggy things."

Mum and Dad looked sadly at Baby Andrew and then miserably at Toffee.

Toffee didn't know where to look.

The vet lifted Baby Andrew down from the table, and Toffee and her family returned home.

Dad sat glumly in the armchair with Baby Andrew curled up at his feet.

"I'm sure he'll be his lovely baby self by the morning," said Mum, placing a bowl of water on the carpet.

"I'm sure Toffee won't have to go," said Dad.

"Yes, we're sure you won't have to go," said Mum, stroking Toffee's head.

"I'm not taking any chances," thought Toffee.

Chapter 2

That night, Mum and Dad tucked Baby Andrew up in his new dog basket.

They were exhausted. They went upstairs to bed and were soon snoring loudly.

Toffee went into action.

She went over to where Baby Andrew was sleeping and gave him a nudge.

Baby Andrew woke up and gave an excited "Woof" when he saw Toffee.

Toffee wagged her tail at Baby Andrew and then scampered into the kitchen.

Baby Andrew scampered after her, just as Toffee hoped he would.

Once inside the kitchen, Toffee pushed the door closed with her nose. She sat down in front of Baby Andrew.

Just as Toffee hoped he would, Baby Andrew sat down in front of Toffee.

Toffee looked at Baby Andrew. Baby Andrew looked at Toffee.

Toffee woofed. Baby Andrew woofed.

Toffee sniffed. Baby Andrew sniffed.

Toffee scratched her left ear. Baby Andrew scratched his left ear.

Toffee stood up on two legs and walked over to the kitchen drawer.

Baby Andrew stood up and followed her.

Toffee took out a bib and placed it over her head and then handed one to Baby Andrew.

She took two breakfast bowls from the shelf, a carton of milk from the fridge, and two breakfast spoons from the drawer.

"Woof!" said Baby Andrew, excitedly.

"Gurgle," said Toffee. "Goo-goo, gurgle, ga-ga google."

Baby Andrew listened carefully and then smiled. "Gurgle," he said. "Goo-goo, gurgle, ga-ga google."

"That's more like it," thought Toffee, climbing into the high chair.

Baby Andrew climbed into the high chair with Toffee. He waited to see what she would do next.

Toffee picked up a breakfast spoon and poured milk and cereal into a bowl. Baby Andrew did the same.

Toffee put a spoonful of crunchy flakes into her mouth.

Baby Andrew did the same.

Toffee reached for some sugar, sprinkled it on her crunchy flakes and gurgled.

Baby Andrew did the same.

Toffee burped.

Baby Andrew burped.

Toffee threw a spoonful on to the floor, just for fun.

Baby Andrew did the same.

Spoonful by spoonful, Toffee emptied her breakfast bowl.

Spoonful by spoonful, Baby Andrew did the same.

Toffee climbed down from the high chair.

Baby Andrew did the same.

Toffee messed about with the fridge magnets. Baby Andrew did the same.

"This is going to work!" thought Toffee. "It's really going to work!"

The next morning, Baby Andrew's mum and dad woke to the sound of loud woof-woof-woofing.

Mum gripped the bed sheets and looked anxiously at Dad.

"Is that Toffee – or is it Baby Andrew barking at the postman?" said Mum.

Mum and Dad crept to the top of the stairs and peered down.

Toffee was sitting on the doormat, wagging her tail excitedly.

Mum and Dad walked down the stairs and patted Toffee on the head.

They then crept into the lounge and closed the door behind them.

Toffee sat outside the door and waited.

Ten minutes later (seventy minutes in doggy years) the lounge door sprang open. Baby Andrew's mum and dad came dancing out.

"Toffee, it's good news! It's fantastic news! Baby Andrew is Baby Andrew again and you don't have to go!" cried Dad.

"Yes! You can stay Toffee!" smiled Mum. "You can stay! Baby Andrew isn't doing doggy things any more! He's doing baby things. He's doing amazing things! He's walking, and gurgling and googling again."

"And guess what, Toffee!" said Dad.

"He can spell 'Doggybix' with the fridge magnets, and he can spell 'walkies' and 'lamp post'. He can even write a whole sentence: '*Top breeders recommend it.*'"

"It's incredible" said Mum, happily.

"It's a miracle!" said Dad.

"Goo-goo-goo, I mean, woof-woof-woof!" said Toffee.

A Cat Too Many

Linda Jennings

Chapter 1

"There's only one not taken," said Mrs Tidy. "That one."

The tabby kitten was tiny, even for two weeks. A scrap of a thing, with a white face.

"Can I pick it up?" asked Nikky.

"Better not," said Mrs Tidy. "It's too small yet."

Mrs Tidy had seven cats, as well as the mother cat and her four kittens. The room smelt of cats and fish, and Nikky's mother wrinkled her nose.

"Perhaps we'll leave it till she's six weeks old. Then we'll come to collect her — " she began, but Nikky tugged at her sleeve.

"No, Mum," she pleaded.

Nikky didn't care about Mrs Tidy's room smelling of cats and fish. She was crazy about cats.

"I wish we had a house like Mrs Tidy's," she said, as they walked home.

"One's quite enough," said Mum. "You'll have to look after it, you know."

"Of course I will," said Nikky. "I know all about worming and grooming, and litter trays and —"

"OK," said Mum, laughing. "I believe you."

They reached their front door. They lived above Jim Mackenzie's corner shop. There was a ginger cat living among the wooden crates on the pavement.

Jim Mackenzie had made a bed for it in a crate marked *Best Apples*. It wasn't his cat, he explained, but it kept the mice away.

Nikky stooped down to look inside the crate and two large, green eyes stared out at her.

When she had first seen him, the cat had spat at her. Now he knew her, and a purr rumbled in his throat.

Nikky knew better than to stroke him, though. Mum had warned her that stray cats had often been badly treated. They might lash out.

"Poor thing," said Nikky. "I wonder if he's got enough to eat?"

"I expect so," said Mum, opening the door. Given half a chance, she knew that Nikky would bring him tins of cat food every day.

Next day, Nikky went with Mum to buy a collar for her new kitten with her pocket money. When they got back, Nikky looked into the crate as usual. The ginger cat stared out at her, green eyes squinting, and spat.

"That's funny, Mum," said Nikky. "He hasn't done that for ages."

"Got out of his crate the wrong side, I expect," said Mum.

"Cat's been like that all morning," said Jim Mackenzie. "It won't let me near it."

Just then, Nikky saw bloodstained paw marks, on the pavement.

"Mum," she shouted. "I think the cat's been hurt."

Gently, Jim pulled the crate towards him. The cat whimpered with pain.

"Car accident, I reckon," said Jim. "But I'm too busy to take it to the vet. It's not really mine, anyway."

Nikky stared at the shopkeeper in horror.

But you can't just leave him!

Jim Mackenzie didn't seem to care.

"It'll be OK. These old strays are tough," he said.

"Come on, Nikky," said Mum. "Jim's right. We can't do anything."

Nobody cares about a poor old cat, without a home, thought Nikky.
As Mum pulled her unwillingly inside, she looked back. She thought she saw a ginger head poking out from the crate, but she couldn't really see through her tears.

Nikky worried about the cat all day.

Mum was worried too, and she told Dad about it. She explained how difficult it would be to catch the cat and take him to the vet.

"You're right, love," said Dad. "He'd probably struggle, and you'd do more harm than good. I expect Jim will ask the RSPCA to put him down."

"Put him down?" Nikky stared at Dad in horror. She knew Mum and Dad weren't crazy about animals. But how could they let the poor cat be killed? She ran into her bedroom, slamming the door.

Then she made up her mind. She would smuggle the cat upstairs to her bedroom. She would look after him, until he was better.

Nikky took her new cat basket from the cupboard. She knew Mum would be cross. But this was an emergency! Very quietly, she slipped down the stairs.

The cat was still there.

His bad leg looked all red and bloody, and flies were buzzing round it. Nikky felt rather sick.

"Come on, Puss," she said quietly, opening the basket.

"Did your Mum send you down, then?" asked Jim Mackenzie, coming over to her.

"Er, no," said Nikky uncomfortably. She couldn't tell him a lie.

But if no one's going to help the poor cat, I am!

"I'd like to know how," said Jim. "Anyway, I've already phoned the RSPCA. They're going to take him away."

Just as Mum and Dad said!

Nikky tipped the crate forward so that the cat would slide out into the cat basket. But before she could do anything, he scrambled out, dragging his wounded leg behind him.

Then he jumped over the wall and into one of the gardens. It must have hurt him terribly.

"Nikky!" Mum came down the stairs. She had seen Nikky talking to Jim. She grabbed her angrily by the arm.

"What do you think you're doing?"

"The cat — " began Nikky, and Mum suddenly shouted at her.

"The cat – that's all you think about, isn't it? Well, let me tell you, if there's any more of this nonsense, you won't even have a kitten!"

Afterwards, Mum was a bit sorry. She sat Nikky down with a drink, and talked to her.

"You don't mean it about the kitten, do you?" asked Nikky. She felt like crying.

"Of course not – but calm down, will you? Try to think of something else but that old cat and the kitten."

That night, Nikky wasn't thinking of her kitten.

She was wondering what would happen if the ginger cat turned up again. How could she stop Jim Mackenzie getting him put down?

Chapter Two

Outside, it had begun to rain. She hoped the cat had found shelter. She hoped that his leg wasn't any worse.

Midow!

What was that?

Nikky's heart began to thump. She opened the window, straining to see outside.

And there it was – a cat with a bad leg, crawling out from the shadows.

Nikky pulled on her dressing gown and dashed out of her bedroom.

Mum! Dad! The cat from downstairs! He's in our garden!

"Nikky, for goodness sake —" began Mum.

"Wait," said Dad. "She may be right. I thought I heard a cat crying. I'll go out and see."

Dad grabbed a torch and hurried downstairs. He opened the back door.

"Well, I never!" he said quietly to Nikky, who had followed behind him. "Just look at this!"

The ginger cat was crouched by the door. He drew back as Dad shone the torch, but he did not run away.

"*Now* what?" said Mum, looking over Dad's shoulder. "You'd better get the RSPCA, Mike. We can't look after it."

"Why not?" Nikky almost shouted.
"We can't let them take him away –
they might put him down – you said
so."

"The RSPCA care about animals,"
said Dad. "They would
only do what was
best for him."

The cat suddenly slid behind them,
crawled upstairs, through the open
door, and into the kitchen. He crouched
in the corner beside the fridge.

"I'll ring them now – there must be
an emergency service," said Dad.

Nikky grabbed hold of his arm. "You *can't* send him away, Dad. He's come to us. He thinks we'll look after him."

"Don't be silly, Nikky, he's only a cat – how can he possibly think anything?"

Nikky crouched down beside the cat, and held out her hand. He snuffled at it with his damp, pink nose. Then he began to purr.

"Dad, look, he trusts me! Don't phone the RSPCA, please."

But Dad was already dialling.

"Hello?" he said.

Nikky gave one big, happy sigh. Dad hadn't phoned the RSPCA. Mr Morgan was the vet!

The vet told Dad to keep the cat warm and dry and to give him fresh water and something to eat.

Mum sighed heavily, as she opened a tin of salmon.

"I hope you know what you're doing," she said.

We can't keep him. Nikky's having the kitten, remember? We haven't got room for two cats.

Nikky watched the cat, as he crawled painfully from the corner and began to nibble at the salmon. He ate daintily, not as if he were hungry at all. He left half of it.

"That's cats for you," said Dad. "Best red salmon, and it turns up its nose."

"It's the shock," said Nikky, who had read all about cats.

And he's probably not used to Salmon.

"I bet not – but that's enough for tonight, Nikky. Off to bed!" said Dad.

Nikky lay for ages thinking about the ginger cat. How funny that he knew she lived upstairs! But what now?

She knew Mum wouldn't change her mind. She didn't like cats much, and they made her sneeze.

At last Nikky fell asleep to the sound of the rain beating against the windowpane.

Next morning, the cat let Dad pick him up and put him in the cat basket.

"He's been someone's pet at some time," said Dad. "You can see that."

"He's a strong cat," said Mr Morgan, when he examined him.

The vet cleaned the wound on the leg, and gave him an injection.

"It's a nasty wound, but there are no bones broken," he said, cheerfully. "Bring him back in four days' time."

Mum looked at the notices on the vet's board. There were lots of people needing cats and kittens.

KITTENS REQUIRED
mmm mm m
mm mmm m
mm mm mm

PLEASE PHONE
PETS PARADISE
11361 2112213

Good home offered for kitten – any colour. phone
Mrs Fluff 01211 011c

Young cat or kitten wanted for children.

Please phone
Mr and Mrs
Cosy. 02034
m mm-.

Kitten – male or female WANTED!!

please phone
Earnest Plee
02013 482143

Nice family offers home to cat – black and white preferred.
Phone 43208 11335

"Good!" she said. "Once his leg's healed, we can put a notice up."

Day by day, the cat's leg grew better. He had a loud, deep purr, and he wound himself round Nikky's legs, and round her heart. She decided to call him Marmalade.

Sometimes, Marmalade would miaow softly at Nikky's bedroom door. And in the morning, Mum would find him curled up on Nikky's duvet.

"I guess the next visit to Mr Morgan will be the last," said Mum. "I'll put a notice on his board."

When no one had replied to the advert within a week, Mum sighed.

Nikky picked up Marmalade and cuddled him. "He's not ugly! He's beautiful," she said. "Anyway, I don't want him to go."

"Nikky," warned Mum. "You know what we said. You can't have a kitten *and* Marmalade."

Nikky knew – and she had a big decision to make.

She went to see her kitten several times. The kitten was still very small, and wobbled round the room after her big, black brother. She had huge eyes and a heart-shaped face. Nikky loved her – but the kitten needed her big brother, and Marmalade needed Nikky.

It was Mrs Tidy who helped Nikky decide.

"The people who want the black kitten would like the tabby one, too," she told Nikky. "I said I didn't think you'd give her up, but —"

Nikky picked up her kitten for the last time, and snuggled it against her neck.

It licked her with a tiny, pink tongue.

"It's all right," she whispered. "They can have her – it will be best, really, seeing she's so small."

She followed Mum out, without looking back. On the way home, Mum bought a new blue collar. The one they'd bought for the kitten would be too small for Marmalade's big neck.

Marmalade was sitting on the doorstep outside the flat, waiting for them. And Nikky could swear there was a smile on his big, square face as he followed them upstairs for his tea.

About the authors

Kes Gray writes:

What gave me the idea for *Crunch Time for Toffee*?

I am not sure, really, except we do have two dogs in our family and the week I wrote this story, our baby daughter Elsie was born.

Dogs and babies? Babies and dogs?

Linda Jennings writes:

Like Nikky, I am mad about cats and I have five of my own.

Unwanted cats can be so sad and this is why I wrote about Marmalade in *A Cat Too Many*.